Dear Parent:
Your child's love of reading starts here!

Every child learns to read in a different way and at his or her own speed. Some go back and forth between reading levels and read favorite books again and again. Others read through each level in order. You can help your young reader improve and become more confident by encouraging his or her own interests and abilities. From books your child reads with you to the first books he or she reads alone, there are I Can Read Books for every stage of reading:

SHARED READING
Basic language, word repetition, and whimsical illustrations, ideal for sharing with your emergent reader

BEGINNING READING
Short sentences, familiar words, and simple concepts for children eager to read on their own

READING WITH HELP
Engaging stories, longer sentences, and language play for developing readers

READING ALONE
Complex plots, challenging vocabulary, and high-interest topics for the independent reader

ADVANCED READING
Short paragraphs, chapters, and exciting themes for the perfect bridge to chapter books

I Can Read Books have introduced children to the joy of reading since 1957. Featuring award-winning authors and illustrators and a fabulous cast of beloved characters, I Can Read Books set the standard for beginning readers.

A lifetime of discovery begins with the magical words **"I Can Read!"**

Visit www.icanread.com for information
on enriching your child's reading experience.

I Can Read® is a trademark of HarperCollins Publishers.

Batman: Going Ape
Copyright © 2012 DC Comics.
BATMAN and all related characters and elements are trademarks of and © DC Comics.
(S12)

HARP2530
Manufactured in China. No part of this book may be used or reproduced in any manner whatsoever without written permission except in the case of brief quotations embodied in critical articles and reviews. For information address HarperCollins Children's Books, a division of HarperCollins Publishers, 195 Broadway, New York, NY 10007.
www.icanread.com

Library of Congress catalog card number: 2011941961
ISBN 978-0-06-188522-8
Book design by John Sazaklis

17 18 SCP 10 9 8 7 ❖ First Edition

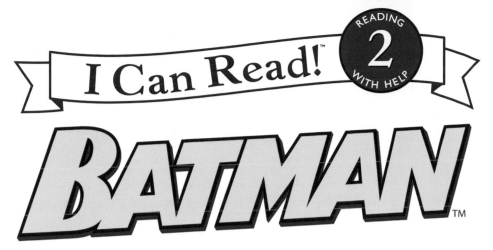

I Can Read!

READING 2 WITH HELP

BATMAN™

Going Ape

by Laurie S. Sutton

pictures by Steven E. Gordon

colors by Eric A. Gordon

BATMAN created by Bob Kane
SUPERMAN created by Jerry Siegel and Joe Shuster

HARPER
An Imprint of HarperCollinsPublishers

BRUCE WAYNE

Bruce Wayne is
a very rich man.
He is secretly Batman.

CLARK KENT

Clark Kent is a newspaper
reporter. He is secretly
Superman.

SUPERMAN

Superman has many amazing
powers. He was born on the
planet Krypton.

BATMAN

Batman fights crime in
Gotham City. He wears
a mask and a cape.

GORILLA
GRODD

Gorilla Grodd
is a very smart
ape. He has the
ability to control
people's minds.

It was a special day at the Gotham City Zoo.

A new ape exhibit was opening.

All the media was there for the big event.

Clark Kent was covering the story for the *Daily Planet*.

Bruce Wayne was also there.

He was a guest of honor.

"ROAR!"

Clark and Bruce turned toward the sound.

An ape had gotten out of his cage!

This was no normal animal.

8

It was Gorilla Grodd!

"Grodd must have let himself be captured to sneak into Gotham," Bruce said.

"We need to stop him," Clark said.

Grodd was very strong and very smart.

He hated humans.

He wanted them to be his slaves.

Grodd had built a special helmet

that he used to control people.

He grabbed a TV cameraman.

"The camera will send my mind waves

to everyone who is watching.

I will take over the world!"

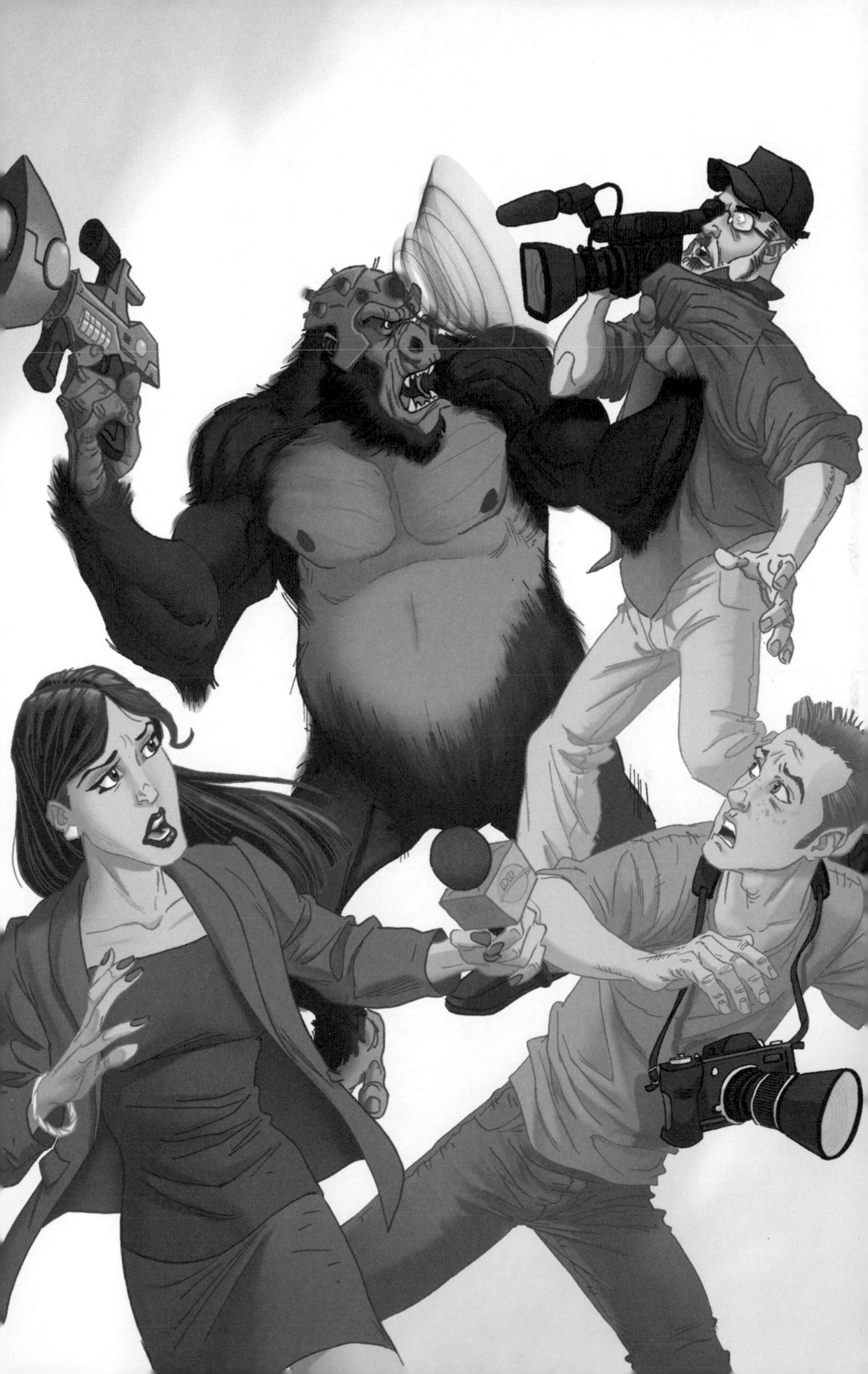

"This is a job for Superman!" Clark said.

"And Batman!" Bruce said.

The two heroes quickly

changed into their costumes.

"Stop this monkey business, Grodd,"
Superman said.

"But I'm just getting started!
I am going to make an army of apes
with my E-Ray," Grodd roared.

Grodd pointed his E-Ray at Batman.

He wanted to make the Caped Crusader

part of his ape army first.

"Batman! Look out!" Superman said.

He jumped in front of his friend.

Superman didn't know

that Grodd had put a kryptonite lens

in the E-ray just for him!

The ray turned Superman into an ape.

"You escaped my E-Ray, Batman,
but you can't get away
from my mind control," Grodd growled.
Batman had a surprise for Grodd.

"My cowl protects me from mind-control waves," Batman said. Grodd roared in anger.

"Get him!" Grodd yelled.

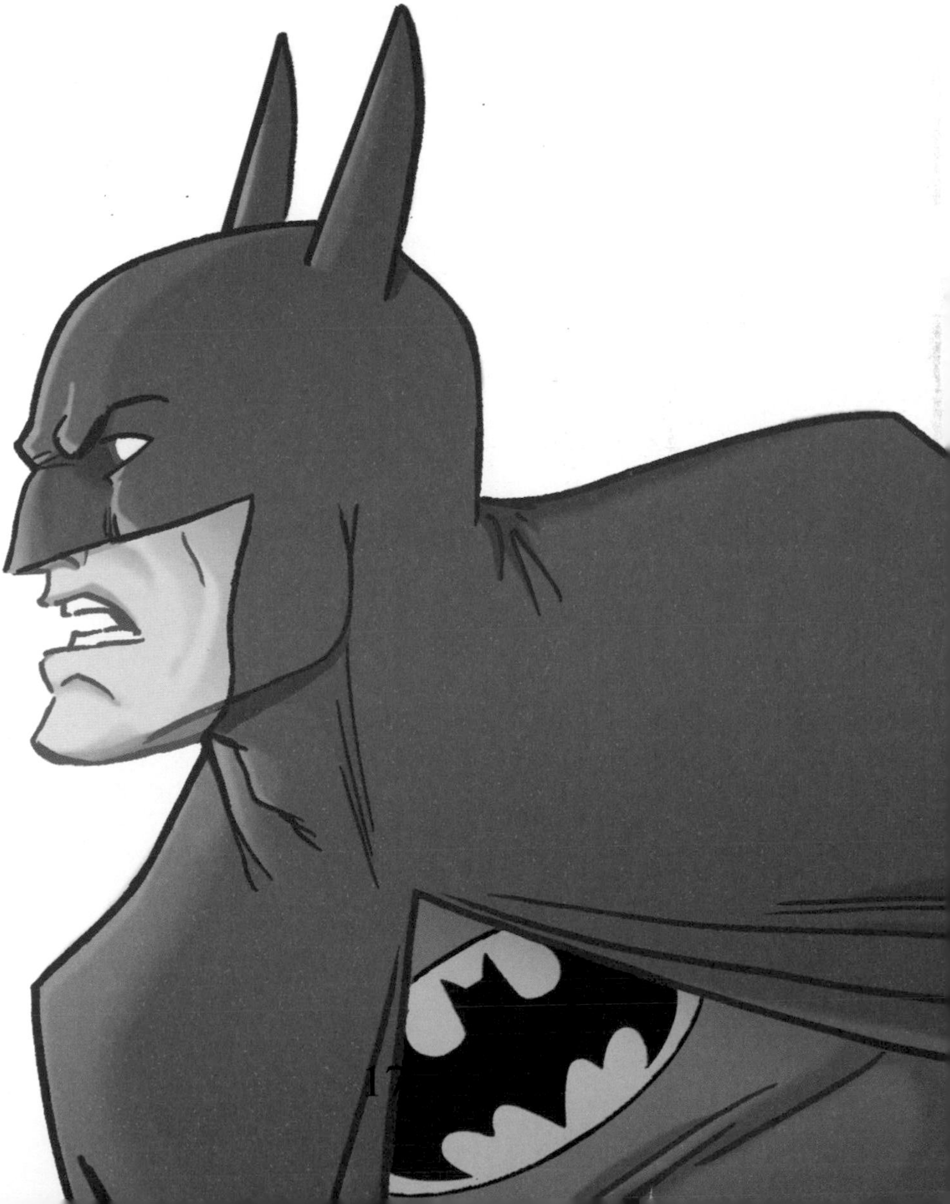

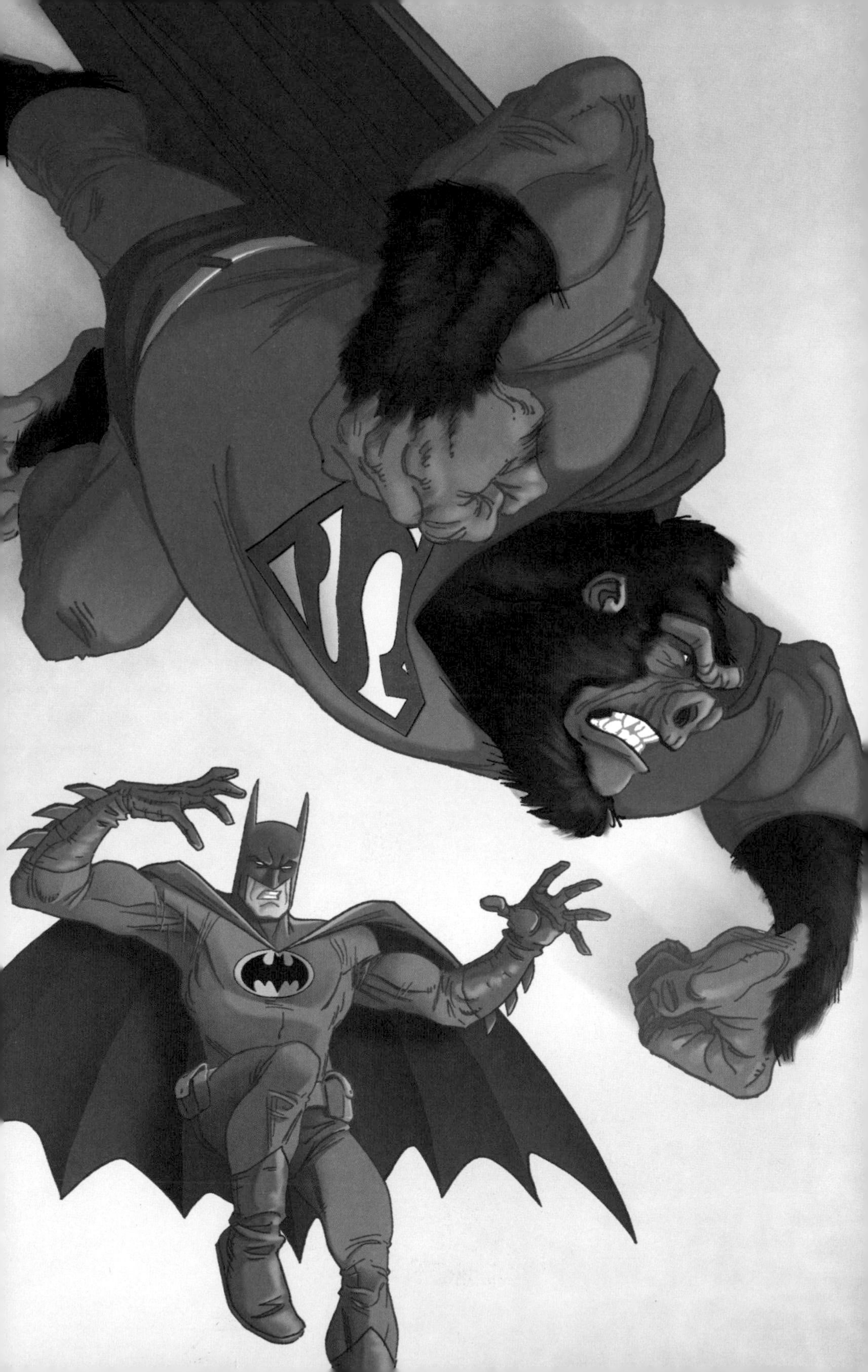

In ape form,

Superman was under Grodd's control.

He charged at Batman.

Batman jumped out of the way.

"How can I stop Superman

without hurting him?"

Batman wondered.

While Batman and Superman fought, Grodd made more apes for his army.

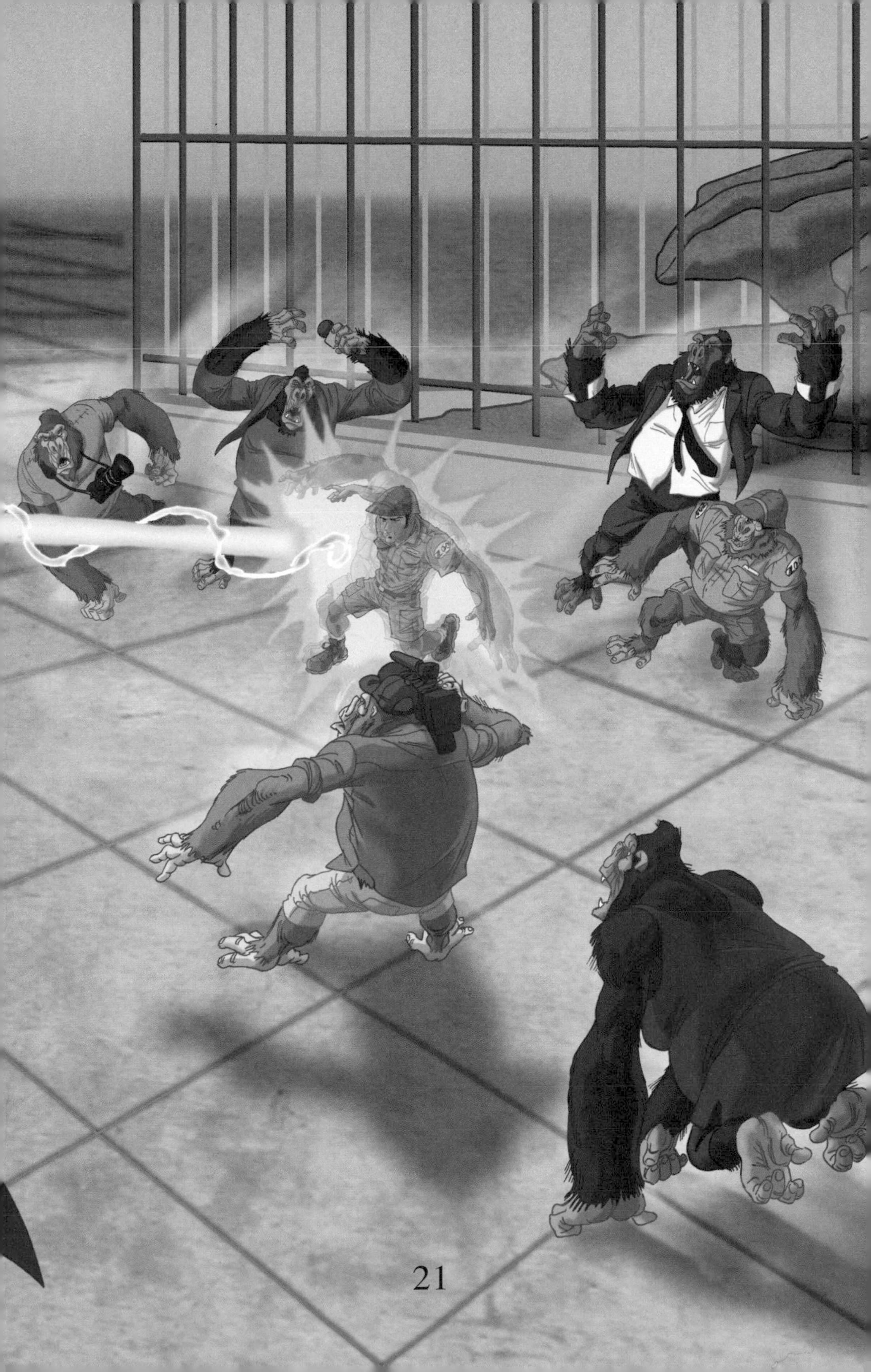

"If I want to end this now," Batman said,

"I'm going to need Superman's help."

He moved between Grodd and Superman.

When Superman charged again,

Batman stepped out of the way.

Superman crashed
into Grodd,
sending the E-Ray flying!

Batman grabbed it with his Batrope.

"If I can fix the wiring,

I can reverse the E-Ray,

but I'd better hurry!" Batman said.

Batman quickly fixed the E-Ray and aimed it at the Man of Steel. "This will make you feel more like yourself," Batman said. With Superman back to normal, Grodd's mind control was gone. "I can think for myself again," Superman said. "Enough monkeying around. Let's cage Grodd."

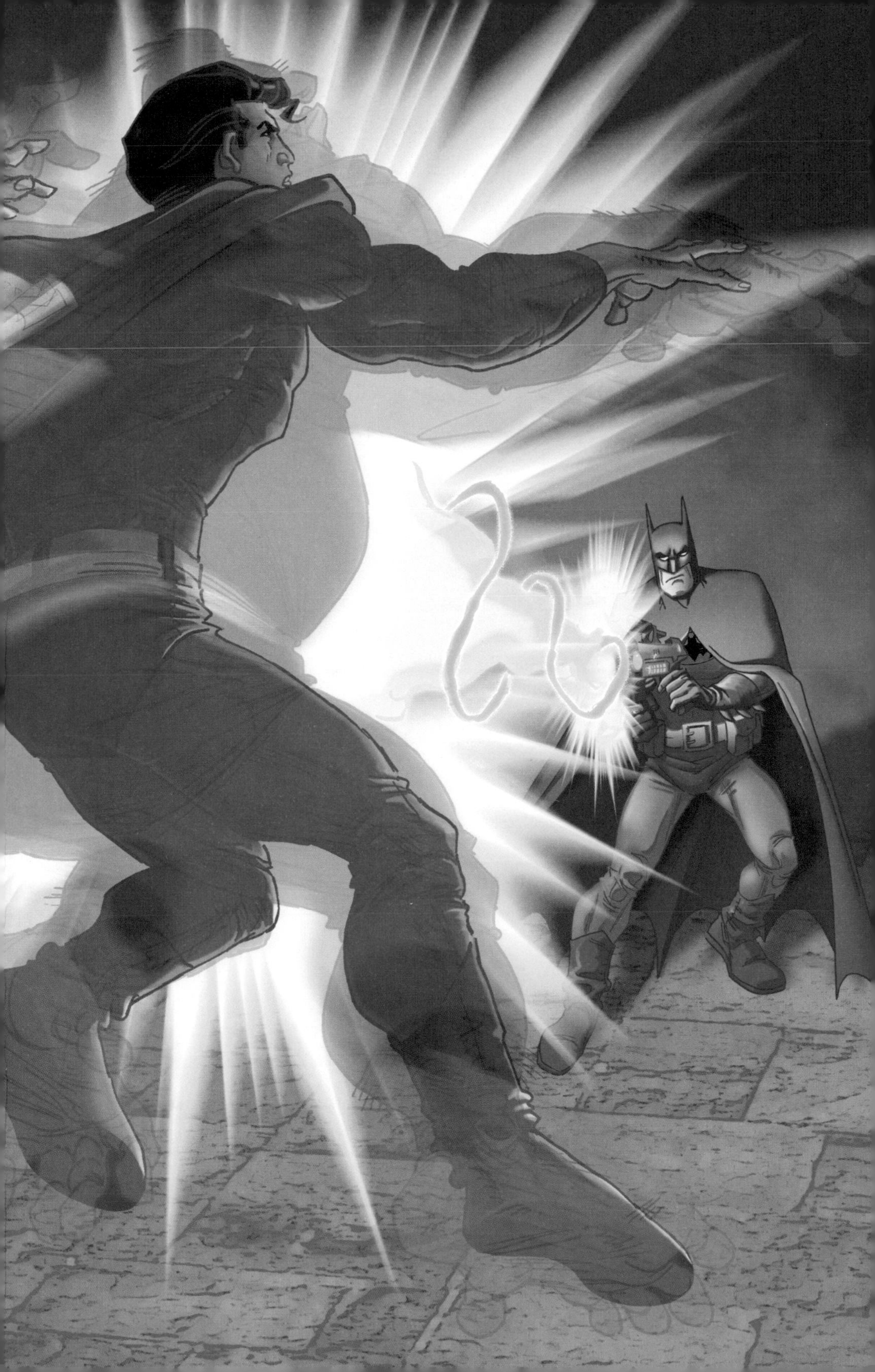

Superman used his heat vision

to melt Grodd's helmet.

Now Grodd could not control his ape army.

"Get Grodd!" the apes yelled.

The only thing Grodd could do

was run away.

The heroes chased Grodd
into the penguin exhibit.
Grodd slipped on the ice.
Batman lassoed Grodd
with his Batrope.

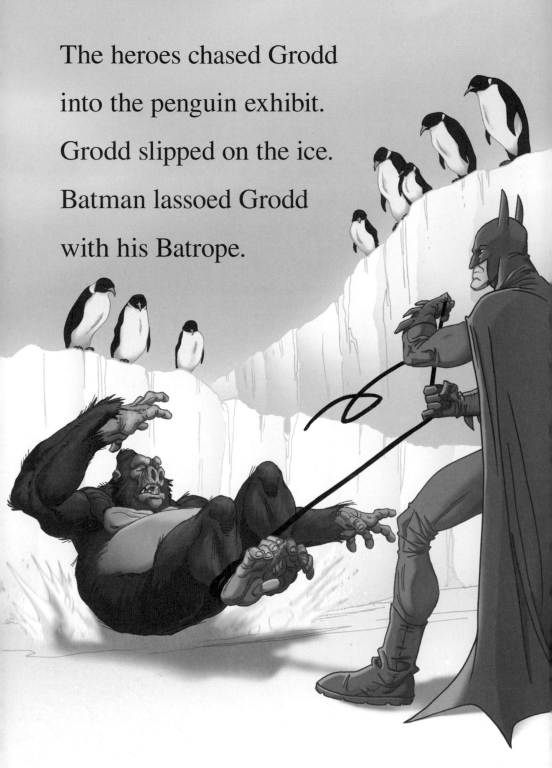

Then Superman used his freezing breath
to make sure the bad guy could not move.

With the help of the zookeepers,

the police took Grodd away.

And Superman and Batman used the E-Ray

to turn the apes back into people.

Gotham City was safe again.